T0196792

TRIAL OF LEE HARVEY OSWALD
LBJ's Patsy

David B. Nolan, Sr.

authorHOUSE®

AuthorHouse™
1663 Liberty Drive
Bloomington, IN 47403
www.authorhouse.com
Phone: 1 (800) 839-8640

Published by AuthorHouse 10/20/2015

ISBN: 978-1-5049-2919-6 (sc)
ISBN: 978-1-5049-2918-9 (e)

Library of Congress Control Number: 2015913072

Print information available on the last page.

*Any people depicted in stock imagery provided by Thinkstock are models,
and such images are being used for illustrative purposes only.
Certain stock imagery © Thinkstock.*

This book is printed on acid-free paper.

By Ira Jefferson "Jack" Beers Jr. (1910-2009) for The Dallas Morning News
(Life time: Originated from the Warren Commission report, a US Government
report. From WH Vol.21 p.19) [Public domain], via Wikimedia Commons

WANTED

FOR

TREASON

THIS MAN is wanted for treasonous activities against the United States:

1. Betraying the Constitution (which he swore to uphold):
   He is turning the sovereignty of the U. S. over to the communist controlled United Nations.
   He is betraying our friends (Cuba, Katanga, Portugal) and befriending our enemies (Russia, Yugoslavia, Poland).
2. He has been WRONG on innumerable issues affecting the security of the U.S. (United Nations-Berlin wall-Missle removal-Cuba-Wheat deals-Test Ban Treaty, etc.)
3. He has been lax in enforcing Communist Registration laws.
4. He has given support and encouragement to the Communist inspired racial riots.
5. He has illegally invaded a sovereign State with federal troops.
6. He has consistantly appointed Anti-Christians to Federal office: Upholds the Supreme Court in its Anti-Christian rulings.
   Aliens and known Communists abound in Federal offices.
7. He has been caught in fantastic LIES to the American people (including personal ones like his previous marraige and divorce).

By Marina Oswald [Public domain], via Wikimedia Commons

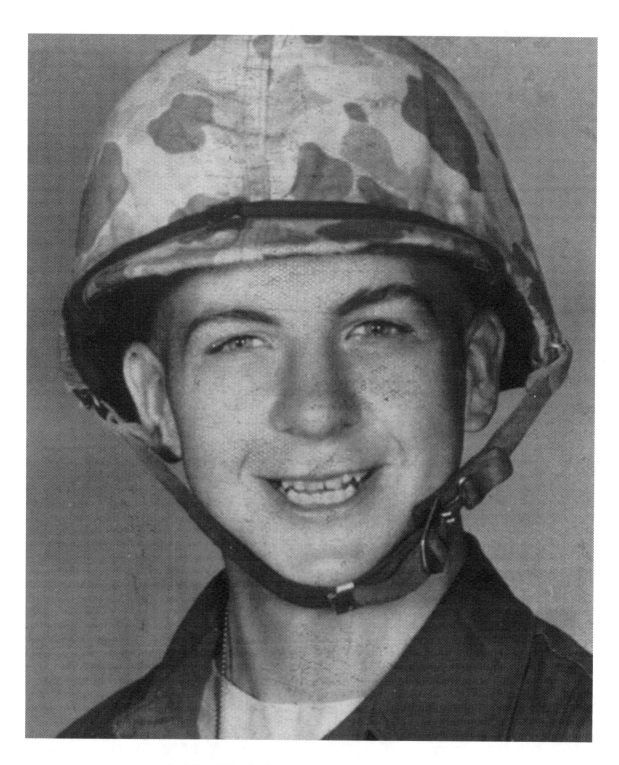

By USMC [Public domain], via Wikimedia Commons

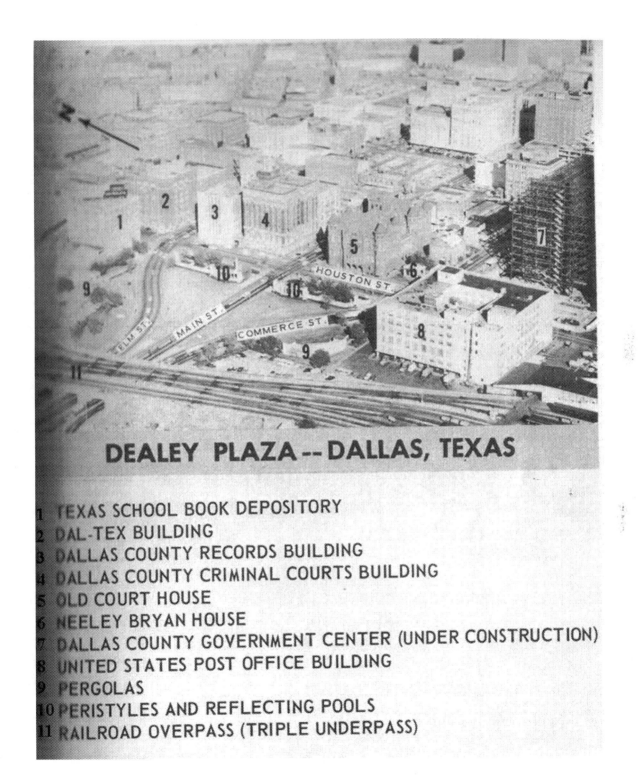

DEALEY PLAZA -- DALLAS, TEXAS

1 TEXAS SCHOOL BOOK DEPOSITORY
2 DAL-TEX BUILDING
3 DALLAS COUNTY RECORDS BUILDING
4 DALLAS COUNTY CRIMINAL COURTS BUILDING
5 OLD COURT HOUSE
6 NEELEY BRYAN HOUSE
7 DALLAS COUNTY GOVERNMENT CENTER (UNDER CONSTRUCTION)
8 UNITED STATES POST OFFICE BUILDING
9 PERGOLAS
10 PERISTYLES AND REFLECTING POOLS
11 RAILROAD OVERPASS (TRIPLE UNDERPASS)

If you believe in the Easter Bunny, the alleged weapons of mass destruction in Iraq, or any refusal of the U.S. federal government to eavesdrop on phone calls from one hundred million Americans, you will be probably believe in the Warren Commission cover up of the assassination of our 35th president, John Fitzgerald Kennedy. Phillip F. Nelson's book, LBJ: The Mastermind of the JFK Assassination persuasively argues that Vice President Lyndon Baines Johnson had the motive, the ruthless power grabbing temperament, and the opportunity to lead the unconstitutional coup d'état to topple the leader of the free world. Authors Roger Stone and ex-patriot Richard Belzer, also reach the same conclusions upon which I expand herein.

Only twenty-one (21%) percent of Americans agree with the Warren Commission conclusion that there was a single assassin of our first and only Catholic U.S. president. Sixty-two medical observers saw entry wound to JFK' right temple entry that resulted in an exit wound that blew out the back third of the president's skull and brains. Seventy-two percent believe in federal government responsibility for the cover up of the assassination. Eighty-two percent believe in some CIA involvement.

The mobster Jack Rudy's murder of Lee Harvey Oswald denied the American public a tribunal to ascertain the truth. My fictional trial consolidates information now in the public domain that the federal government does not want you to know regarding the involvement of the CIA, the FBI, the U.S. Secret Service, the Dallas Police, the U.S. military, and the highly discredited Warren Commission.

Jack and his brother Robert Kennedy, the U.S. Attorney General, knew of the criminal investigation of LBJ and his cronies Billy Sol Estes and Bobby Baker for corruption. JFK decided by summer 1963 that LBJ had to be dumped from the 1964 Democratic Party ticket to further Jack Kennedy's re-election. North Carolina Governor, Terry Sanford, was to replace Johnson on the Democratic ticket.

LBJ knew that his political career would be soon over and his imprisonment would follow. LBJ's only out was to lead a coup d'état to commit treason with the murder of his president.

In October 1963, JFK fired Alan Dulles as the CIA Director. After his expected 1964 re-election, Kennedy planned to make his brother Robert the CIA Director. Bobby was then to "clean house" to present another Bay of Pigs invasion disaster. By November 22, 1963, the Military Industrial Complex had other ideas. With JFK out of the way, the Viet Nam War could escalate for the profits of the merchants of war and the insatiable ego of LBJ, the treasonous Yellow Rat of Texas.

As LBJ's limousine entered the Dealey Plaza, the "vice" president nervously ducked to the floor of the vehicle leaving his own wife, Lady Bird Johnson, and Texas political adversary, Senator Lloyd Benson exposed to the anticipated rifle fire to come soon. Such bizarre behavior confirms LBJ's own foreknowledge and complicity in what in 1976 the U.S. Congress concluded was a conspiracy of shooters from both the Texas School Book Repository and the grassy knoll at Dallas's Dealey

Plaza. The Executive and Judicial branches of the U.S. Government have hidden this truth from the American people for over one - half century.

The coward LBJ used a pretext as a New Guinea flight observer to feign a politically orchestrated Silver Star medal for himself while a Capitol Hill staffer. LBJ cowered behind Lady Bird's skirts in Dealey Plaza so as later to send 67,000 brave American troops to their deaths in Indo China for the financial gain of his cronies.

Before his death, Jack Kennedy decided to remove all U.S. advisors and troops from the unwinnable Viet Nam War. As part of LBJ's unholy deal for his power ascendency, the new U.S. president sent over one half million troops to face death in Southeast Asia. This is the LBJ legacy as the most corrupt and disastrous president in U.S. history.

The brother of the Dallas Police Chief in late 1963 was the former Deputy CIA Director. Dallas police were told to face the Kennedy motorcade rather than to observe open windows for potential snipers along the JFK limousine route. Rogue elements of the Dallas police and the U.S. Secret Service signed off on the parade route that brought the president slowly through the sniper nests at Dealey Plaza in downtown Dallas, Texas. The Kennedy limousine slowed to 5 MPH as it made its turn in front of the grassy knoll at the rail road under pass.

LBJ took no chances. His personal assassin, Malcolm "Mac" Wallace, was stationed on the sixth floor of the Texas School Book Depository. Mac left his finger print near the shooter's window from which JFK received two shots. Wallace later died mysteriously from "carbon monoxide poisoning" while driving. Sniper Charles Harrelson confessed to shooting JFK from the grassy knoll. Harrelson, involved in as many as twenty mob hits and was later convicted of shooting fatally a federal judge.

Over seventy mobsters and others with knowledge of the details of the JFK assassination have died in mysterious circumstances over the last half century. On his deathbed, CIA operative, E. Howard Hunt, confessed to his participation in the LBJ planned murder to JFK.

The Trial of Lee Harvey Oswald (c)

By David B. Nolan,
BA, MPA, J.D.
97 Willow Run Drive
Centerville, MA 02632-2421
571-277-3265

Military Tribunal at Guantanamo Bay (GITMO)

Presiding Judge: Earl Warren

Special Prosecutor: Arlen Spector (Warren Commission staff apologist)

Defense Counsel: David Brian Nolan (U.S. Supreme Court litigator)

Opening Argument by the Federal Government

This military tribunal will establish beyond a reasonable doubt that defendant Lee Harvey Oswald was the sole assassin in the death our 35th president, John F. Kennedy, on November 22, 1963. There is no cover up or obstruction of justice by President Lyndon Baines Johnson, FBI Director J. Edgar Hoover, or Supreme Court Chief Justice Earl Warren. There are no facilitating rogue elements of the CIA, the U.S. Secret Service, the FBI, the Dallas Police, and U.S. Military Intelligence to frame Lee Harvey Oswald as a "patsy" for the murder of JFK and police officer J.D. Tippet.

On November 22, 1963 there was no prohibition under United States Code that made the murder of a sitting president a federal crime. Moreover, there can be no criminal conspiracy upon proof that Lee Harvey Oswald was a lone nut.

Defendant Oswald *de facto* resigned his U.S. Citizenship when he sought and received his passport from the Union of Soviet Socialist Republics (USSR). Mr. Oswald should be treated in this trial as a non-Islamic terrorist who is not entitled to due process protection under the United States Constitution.

The following facts and foundation of witnesses have been stipulated to in this proceeding.

This specially established military court has jurisdiction to determine that war criminal Oswald deprived the Chief of our Armed Services of his civil rights, including JFK's own life. I allege that Defendant Oswald fatally wounded President Kennedy by inflicting three rifle wounds, including the "magic bullet", from his sniper nest in the 6th floor of the Texas School Book Depository which overlooked the presidential motorcade traveling through the Dealey Plaza in Dallas, Texas. His murder weapon was ordered through the mail by a "Alek J. Hidell" and found on the fifth floor of the Depository. The British Enfield and German Mauser rifles found on the 6th Floor are irrelevant to the "single shooter" I allege in this matter

The Government will take testimony today from each of the three key witnesses who testified before the Warren Commission. Their statements remain sworn today. At the end of the prosecution's case, I will move for admission to the trial record the same two evidentiary items already admitted by the Warren Commission Report. These are three pubic hairs of Lee Harvey Oswald and the dental records of Jack Ruby's (Jack Rubenstein's) mother.

The U.S. Government also has Mr. Oswald by the short hairs despite terrorist Oswald unfortunately survived assassination himself by Jack Ruby's single shot. I ask that this Court rubber stamp all findings of the Warren Commission that included Minority House Leader and future unelected president, Gerald R. Ford, the Chief Justice Warren of the United States, and the former CIA Director Allen Dulles that JFK fired a month before his death.

Prosecution's first witness: Howard Berman

Please state your name for the record?

Howard Berman.

What is your occupation?

I am a pipe fitter in Dallas, Texas.

Were you present at Dealey Plaza on November 22, 1963?

Yes. I was having lunch on Elm Street immediately across the street from the Texas School Book Depository Building.

Did you observe anything at this time?

I heard what I thought was a backfire. It ran in my mind that it might be someone throwing fire crackers out of nearby the red brick building. I looked up.

I saw the defendant Oswald leaning out of a corner window of the Texas School Book Depository with a rifle. As the motorcade passed, I saw Oswald aim, fire and hit president Kennedy with his high-powered rifle. I saw Oswald smirk with satisfaction on his third and fatal shot.

Do you see Lee Harvey Oswald in the court room today?

Yes, but he is not smirking now. He looks already dead.

Cross examination by Defense Counsel

Did the Warren Commission base any of its findings on your proffered testimony that you again state under oath today?

No.

Did you fail to identify Lee Harvey Oswald in a police lineup on the day of the assassination?

Yes.

How do you know that this shooter you saw was using a "high –powered" rifle?

I don't know nothing about rifles.

Would it surprise you to learn that a high-powered rifle shoots more than 2600 feet per second?

I don't know.

Would it surprise you that Mr. Oswald does not own or possess a high-powered rifle that would cause a three inch hole in the back of the president's skull?

Yes.

Prosecution's second witness: Helen Markam

Please state your name for the record?

Helen Markham.

Do you recognize defendant Oswald in the court room?

Yes.

Have you seen him in person previously?

Yes

When was that?

I saw him on November 22, 1963 approximately forty-five minutes after the shooting of the president.

Where did you see Mr. Oswald?

I saw the defendant walk up to Officer Tippet's patrol car window and speak to the policeman. I saw Oswald then shoot J.D. Tippet three times through the police car open window. I then carried on a twenty minute conversation with the dying policeman.

Prosecution: I have no further questions.

Cross examination by Defense Counsel

Did you fail to identify defendant Oswald during each of eight police line ups?

Yes. But I identified him in the ninth lineup.

Would you be surprised to learn that police officer J.D. Tippet died instantly from four shots through a closed police car window?

Yes.

Why did you place your shoes on the top of officer Tippet's patrol car?

I don't remember.

Would you be surprised to learn that none of the bullets recovered from officer Tippet's body, i.e. three-copper coated Westerns and one lead Remington can be traced to defendant Oswald's 38 caliber revolver?

Yes. Maybe officer Tippet already had a fourth bullet in his body.

Would you be surprised to learn that an investigating Dallas officer marked each of the four cartridges at the scene with his initials but later these markings were nowhere to be found after being placed in FBI custody?

Yes. I don't know why there would be evidence tampering by the FBI.

Prosecution's third witness: Marina Oswald

I now call my third witness, Marina Oswald.

Please state your name for the record?

Marina Oswald. I am Mrs. Lee Harvey Oswald.

Do you recognize in the courtroom Lee Harvey Oswald?

Yes. He my husband.

Is he a violent man against you or others?

Nyet. Lee good man. Lee never shoot anyone.

Are you a communist sympathizer?

No. I want our daughters and me to remain in America.

Is your husband a communist sympathizer?

No. He is an American patriot and a proud Marine intelligence operative.

Did your husband ever hit you?

I don't remember.

Why did you marry Lee?

My uncle gave me the choice of marrying Lee or another U.S. spy sent to Russia. I chose Lee since he was in Minsk already and I did not have to move several hundred miles away. If Lee dies, I will marry an FBI agent or someone else to protect our daughters.

Cross examination by Defense Counsel

Have federal authorities held you in custody for several weeks after the presidential assassination?

Yes.

Have you been threatened with deportation?

Yes. But I will soon be married to an FBI agent.

Does your husband have any reason to kill the president?

No.

Was your husband a U.S. Intelligence officer when he entered the Soviet Union?

Yes.

Did he attempt to infiltrate a conspiracy to kill the president?

Yes.

Prosecution's fourth witness: Dr. Renatus Hartogs

Please state your name and expertise?

Dr. Renatus Hartogs. I was the Warren Commission's psychiatrist.

What is your professional opinion regarding Lee Harvey Oswald?

I examined Lee when he was a troubled thirteen year- old. I believe that his repressed oedipal lust for his mother engendered overwhelming feelings of guilt. This was his murder motivation.

The coincidence of the triad of three shots into both the president and into Officer J.D. Tippet project the assassin's penis and gonads.

Defense Cross-examination

Would it surprise you that four bullets were retrieved from the corpse of officer Tippet?

If so, I believe that three of these four bullets must be from the same weapon, Lee' figurative penis. The shots towards the president were through the "vaginal" open window of the Texas School Book Repository in Oedipal theory first raised by Sigmund Freud.

The government and I have stipulated to the introduction of the following actual exhibits from the Warren Commission: (1) a detailed analysis of each of defendant's three pubic hairs and, (2) the 1938 dental chart of Jack Ruby's mother.

Judge Warren: Motion approved.

<u>The prosecution rests.</u>

<u>The Defense moves for dismissal of all charges against Defendant Oswald for the Government's failure to establish any credible motive or factual basis to prove beyond a reasonable doubt of any crime by Lee Harvey Oswald.</u>

Judge Warren: I deny the Defense motion based upon the fact that non-Islamic terrorist Oswald is not entitled to any due process protections under the U.S. Constitution. He has no right to be tried by a domestic court or its rules. His legal defense may now proceed to submit its case to me.

<u>The Defense Opening Statement</u>

Our deceased President Kennedy correctly opined the following:

"We seek a free flow of information… We are not afraid to entrust the American people with unpleasant facts, foreign ideas, alien philosophies, and competitive values. For a nation that is afraid to let its people know the truth and falsehood in an open market is a nation that is afraid of its people." This trial will attempt to determine the truth of the Kennedy assassination.

The prosecution has failed to prove beyond a reasonable doubt that Lee Harvey Oswald was the lone assassin of President John Fitzgerald Kennedy. He was in the third floor snack room of the Texas School Book Depository. He had no gun powder residue on his body upon his arrest. He could not have fired a single shot form any fire arm. Upon his arrest, his recorded voice print showed no stress or attempt to deceive.

Lee Harvey Oswald is a patsy. Similarly, Defendant Oswald did not commit murder of Officer Tippet or any other offense under federal or Texas state law.

Eighty-five percent of Americans disbelieve there was a single shooter at the Dealey Plaza in Dallas, Texas. Three shots cannot be dispensed from the Mannlicher-Carbano, World War I bolt action rifle, in the 2.3 seconds as established in the Abraham Zapruder film taken at Dealey Plaza on November 22, 1963.

Defendant Oswald did not deny any federal civil right to President Kennedy nor violate any other federal or state privilege. Oswald liked JFK. He had no motive to murder JFK.

Defendant Oswald did not commit any prohibited personnel practice under Title V of the United States Code to our federal employee president. Oswald, as a Military Intelligence Officer, did not violate any section of the Uniform Military Code regarding his Commander in Chief.

Defendant Oswald is not charged with conspiracy to violate the law with any other person. However, the Warren Commission members appointed by President Lyndon Baines Johnson have concluded that Mr. Oswald is a lone assassin. No co-conspirator, let alone LBJ who solely benefited from the JFK murder, was found.

The testimony to be presented herein does confirm JFK assassination collusion with organized crime, by President Lyndon Baines Johnson, Chief Justice Earl Warren, and rogue elements of the CIA, FBI, U.S. Secret Service, and the Dallas Police. Oswald was not part of this conspiracy, only its "patsy." Defendant Oswald was framed for killing our 35th president in the eyes of the American public and world opinion until his day in the Court. The French and Russian foreign services each concur in this conclusion.

Defendant Oswald does not have to prove in this trial which actors conspired to commit treason and colluded to obstruct justice in a cover up after the president's assassination. He is innocent of such collusion. He actually attempted to infiltrate the conspiracy to save the president's life.

Defendant Oswald does not have to prove that both Richard Nixon and FBI Director J. Edgar Hoover met with LBJ in Dallas on the day before the assassination. Mr. Oswald does not have to prove that Richard Nixon met with organized crime figures on the day before the assassination. We do not have to prove that LBJ partied the night before with Texas business men to celebrate the coup d'état for the following day.

Defendant Oswald does not have to prove that president Johnson had the JFK motor cade limousine altered to obscure the fact of different bullet type fragments and indentations from as many as eleven projectiles, the shots of which were each recorded on police radio tape. There is physical evidence of rifle bullets from more than one shooter's nest direction. Defendant Oswald need only show that the government's prosecution has failed beyond a reasonable doubt to prove he assassinated the president or Officer J.D. Tippet as charged.

Four million tourists visit yearly the grave of assassinated President of John F. Kennedy at Arlington National Cemetery. Perhaps over two hundred books will be written over a half century about JFK's murder including the best sellers "Killing Kennedy" by Bill O'Reilly, "Dead Wrong" by Richard Belzer, by "The Case Against LBJ" by Roger Stone, and "LBJ: The Mastermind of the JFK Assassination" by Phillip F. Nelson. However, many questions remain unanswered and the Warren Commission conclusions are each universally discredited. Four books have identified LBJ's mastermind role.

Mafioso Jacob Rubenstein, aka Jack Ruby, failed by sheer luck in his assassination attempt of Lee Harvey Oswald in the Dallas Police Headquarters basement with a single shot to Oswald's stomach. Defendant Oswald fortunately received transport in the waiting vehicle for immediate medical attention in a hospital instead of prolonged CPR by Dallas police until near death. The Dallas police failed to delay immediate life- saving hospital treatment through "police resuscitation" to the injured chest. The Trauma Room 1 of the Lakeland Hospital in Dallas had the ability to save the life of Oswald as had it saved the life of severely injured Texas Governor, John Connally, two days before.

Oswald now stands accused of the murders of President John F. Kennedy and Dallas Police Officer J.D. Tippet. This judicial proceeding will probe the possible involvement of the Mafia and rogue elements of the federal government in the assassination and later cover up of important details regarding the death of our 35th president and Officer J.D. Tippet.

We now know that the successor president, Lyndon Baines Johnson, ordered that Kennedy's limousine be altered one week after its fatal drive through the Dealey Plaza, in Dallas, Texas. This destruction prevented further confirmation of two or more different directional origins and copper jacket and non-copper jacket rifle fragments that were recovered from the vehicle. The physical evidence of more than one weapon and the existence at least two sniper nest origins on November 22, 1963 at the Dealey Plaza confirms conspiracy and not a lone assassin.

Seventy-five (75) percent of Americans believes that there were at least two shooters in the assassination of President John Kennedy. In 1979, the U.S. Congress concluded that at least a second sniper from the grassy knoll adjacent to the Elm Street railroad overpass participated in the crime of the 20th Century. Three mobsters, including Sam Giancana, who had ties to the Kennedy assassination were themselves murdered when called to testify before Congress. Giancana and JFK shared the same mistress, Judith Exner.

The U.S. government has spent one-half trillion dollars since the September 11, 2001 Islamic terrorist attack on the World Trade Center. This allocation was used for the Pentagon to hunt down Al Qaeda leader, Osama Bin Laden, and shoot him in the face rather than capture and remove him for trial.

How much has been spent over the last half century to investigate those who conspired to hide the truth from the American people about who killed JFK and orchestrated the assassination cover up? Is there anything in the much maligned Warren Commission Report that is credible today?

The Warren Commission concluded that only three (3) rifle bullets were fired, each from a bolt action, Italian World War I, Mannlicher –Carcano rifle. However, as many as eleven (11) shots were recorded on digital tape from a police motor cycle radio from the Dealey Plaza on November 22, 1963. Medical records reflect that four (4) bullets entered the body of the murdered president, two from the front and two from the back. The Warren Commission only recognized three shots, including the "magic" bullet to both JFK and Governor Connally in violation of the laws of physics.

The two frontal shots to Kennedy's forehead and to his neck each confirm a second shooter from the grassy knoll. The fatal frontal explosive bullet in conical fashion blew out the back third of the president's skull and brain. These shots could not come from the Texas School Book Depository from behind the president's limousine. The first shot was slowed through the presidential limousine wind shield and lodged in JFK's throat without hitting the spine.

Fifty-one (51) witnesses heard the shots from behind the fence at the grassy knoll above Elm Street at the Dealey Plaza in Dallas Texas. Forty (40) witnesses heard the shots from the School Book Depository. Even the federal government's assassination museum in Dallas has a photograph of witnesses diving to the ground to duck shots from behind them on the grassy knoll adjacent to the rail road underpass.

FBI wire taps have recorded confessions of four mobsters regarding that fateful day. The key mafia leader, Giancana, was himself murdered shortly before this gangster was to testify before Congress in 1979 regarding the JFK murder. Giancana received one shot to the back of his head and five shots around his mouth as a warning to others to not disclose the truth.

Confessed Dealey Plaza participants, John Roselli and Chuck Nicoletti, were also murdered just prior to their scheduled testimony before Congress. Roselli confessed to Bill Bonanno about being on a four member hit team in Dallas on November 22, 1963. The CIA had previously recruited Roselli to assassinate Fidel Castro prior to the 1960 fall election that elected John F. Kennedy as president.

Following his conviction for the murder of a federal judge, mobster hitman Charles Harrelson confessed to being a shooter from the grassy knoll at Dealey Plaza. Perhaps for concern for the promising acting career of his son, Buddy, the convicted assassin recanted the JFK murder.

Lee Harvey Oswald's videotaped answers to Dallas police questioning show no voice imprint stress. His statement, "I have killed no one. I am a patsy" is truthful in its content without any deception.

Supreme Court Justice Earl Warren has opined, "You may never get the truth, and I mean that seriously." What does that say about the Warren Commission's failure to investigate fully?

The marble motto above the U.S. Supreme Court main entrance states, "Equal Justice for All." JFK and Oswald appear to be exceptions regarding this promise to the American people. If JFK had ever committed high crimes and misdemeanors, he should have been impeached by the House of Representatives and tried by the U.S. Senate, not murdered.

CIA operative, E. Howard Hunt, made the death bed confession that President Lyndon Johnson coordinated the assassination-which the sociopathic VP code named "The Big Event." By his own Texas bootstraps, the poor-born Johnson jumped from being scorned as a powerless "Cornpone" Vice President to the "Big Time" leader of the free world.

Texas Governor John Connally was severely wounded twice riding in the presidential limousine on November 22, 2013 from the pristine "magic bullet." His shooting and likely death was of no consequence to Lee Oswald, the CIA, FBI, U.S. Secret Service, Dallas police, or Military Intelligence. However, he was a major rival of LBJ for the financial and political control of their Texas Democratic Party base. LBJ tried to get his other key political rival, Texas Senator Ralph Yarborough, also into JFK's limousine for the turkey shoot in Dealey Plaza.

JFK and his very insecure vice president spent fewer than two hours together in year 1963. The Kennedy White House elite called LBJ "Uncle Cornpone" behind his back because of his Texas Hill Country accent and crude manners. LBJ bragged to having more out of marriage sexual relations, "dictation with six of eight White House Secretaries," than the now infamous Tom Cat, Jack.

Johnson especially resented Bobby Kennedy's Harvard education and arrogance. LBJ called the young U.S. Attorney General in only his thirties a "snot nosed kid." Johnson insulted Bobby's manhood when the slender Attorney General was knocked over by rifle recoil when Johnson took him hunting on his ranch. Bobby Kennedy had to be killed later to prevent his becoming president to have the power to unravel the murder conspiracy that killed his brother.

LBJ fired Bobby as attorney general soon after LBJ seized power for the former's protection. This was after the Attorney General made a specific inquiry to the CIA Director about the role of a rogue CIA element in his brother's assassination.

The Warren Commission failed to investigate who ordered several mafia shooters to be present at the Dealey Plaza. It cleverly continued the setup of Oswald, an alleged disgruntled former marine, as the sole assassin.

Lyndon Johnson is the second U.S. vice president that sought a treasonous power grab. Aaron Burr narrowly missed conviction for treason for his violation of the U.S. Constitution that he also swore to defend. Burr failed to start a new country in the western U.S. territories. The ambitious Texan Johnson stole the United States Empire. Ruthless Roman soldier emperors routinely murdered their predecessor when the chance arose after a couple of years.

Former KGB agents Andropov and Putin used their Intelligence network alliances to gain and retain power domestically and internationally. Many believe that Andropov, like Kennedy, died from assassination with the assistance of his authorized body guard protectors.

Dwight David Eisenhower, George H.W. Bush, George W. Bush and Barack Hussein Obama each rose to power with support from Wall Street and the Military Industrial Complex. Bush Sr., president #41, ran the CIA under President Nixon. Junior, president #43, needed support in a Florida recount with 7 to 2 Supreme Court complicity. His contrived Iraq War for Halliburton profit has been a disaster.

Many have questioned whether John McCain (born in Colon, Panama) or Barack Obama (born in Mombossa, Kenya) are both natural born U.S. citizens under U.S. Constitution and statutory requirements. Did Obama under federal law renounce U.S. citizenship in order to travel to Pakistan on an Indonesian passport as a college student? Was he involved with the CIA like his respective maternal grandfather, a former CIA station chief in Lebanon and maternal grandmother, a Honolulu banker for CIA operations? Was Obama's Indonesian Colonel Stepfather part of an Indonesian coup d'état in favor of the pro U.S. Sukarna over the left leaning Sukarno?

Could either 2008 major party candidate for president be removed from power in a bloodless coup by the U.S. Supreme Court and CIA for not being a naturalized U.S. citizen?

The past is prologue.

First Defense Witness: Madeliene Brown

Please state your name for the record.

Madeliene Brown

Were you in Dallas in November 22, 1963?

Yes.

I what capacity was that?

I attended a party of Texas businessmen with Lyndon. I was Lyndon's mistress at the time.

What was the purpose of the party?

It was to celebrate Lyndon's becoming president the following day.

Is that what Lyndon Johnson told you?

I will never forget his exact words. "After tomorrow, these goddamn Kennedys will never embarrass me again. That's no threat. That's a promise".

Prosecution: Objection hearsay !!!

Judge Warren: Objection sustained. Oswald is on trial here, not President Johnson or Sirhan Sirhan.

Why did your lover hate Jack and Bobby Kennedy?

Jack and his brother Bobby called Lyndon "Uncle Cornpone" behind his back.

Whom did your lover say was responsible for the murder of his predecessor?

On New Year's Eve in 1963 at the Driscoll Hotel in Austin, Lyndon told me, "Texas oil mem and intelligence bastards in Washington" had been responsible for the assassination.

Could Lyndon have stopped the snipers at Dealey Plaza in Dallas?

No, he wanted to be President of the United States.

Did Lyndon tell you that he ducked down in the Vice Presidential limousine before it entered the Dealey Plaza?

Yes. He was afraid that a stray bullet for Senator Yarbrough riding in the back seat with him and Lady Bird might hit him. He did not care about his wife getting shot because he would inherit her money and TV station in Austin.

Would Lyndon want Yarbrough dead along with both Jack Kennedy and Governor John Connally?

Yes. Lyndon felt that they were all in his way politically. He wanted Yarbrough to ride with Jack and John. He only needed Jackie to be alive for the swearing in pictures and to be seen with him on the flight back to Washington.

Second Defense Witness: Margerita Oswald

Please state your name for the record?

Margerita Oswald

What is your relationship with the defendant?

I am his mother.

Have you had prior contact with the Federal Bureau of Investigation?

Yes

What is the nature of that contact?

I complained that the federal government was using multiple "Lee Harvey Oswald" identifies as doppelgangers for my son that would undermine his role as an intelligence officer for the U.S. government.

How do you know that there are multiple impostors for your son?

Upon his enlistment with the U.S. marines, Lee was five foot, eleven inches in height with a slim build. One impostor in Mexico City, heavy set with a height of five foot, six inches, with a different wire tapped voice as confirmed by FBI Director, J. Edgar Hoover.

Is your son a patsy to blame as the sole assassin of the president?

Yes. I told this to TV journalist Bob Schaefer on our ride from Fort Worth to Dallas before Lee's murder.

Did Dallas policemen try to save your son after the shooting by Jack Ruby?

No. The single bullet to Lee's stomach adversely affected his spleen, liver, pancreas, and right kidney. Instead of immediately placing him on the readied vehicle for a trip to the Parkland Hospital, the Dallas police attempted "resuscitation." I understand that their imposed chest compression is adverse to any stomach gunshot wound.

Should the Dallas police have treated your son, their prize suspect, better?

This young man, whether he's my son or a stranger, repeatedly declared, "I didn't do it. I didn't do it." And he is shot down. That is not the American way of life. A man is innocent until he is proven guilty.

Third Defense Witness: Nicholas Katsenbach

Can you state your name for the record?

Nicholas Katzenbach, former Acting U.S. Attorney General

Can you identify for the record Defendant's proposed Exhibits?

Yes. These are each Department of Justice official photographs that have been in our Department's continuous possession.

Do you corroborate the testimony so far and the defense introductory statement provided today?

Yes.

The first photo shows a rifle entry wound in President Kennedy's throat at the knot level of his tie. The second photograph shows the measuring of the distance between two rifle wounds to President Kennedy's back. The third photograph shows a rifle wound to the President's right temple that blew out the back third of his skull and brain. The fourth photograph shows Charles Harrelson and two other "clean shaven" bums, possibly Frank Sturgis and E. Howard Hunt, arrested near the grassy knoll and quickly released. The Fifth photograph shows Charles Harrelson upon his arrest for killing a federal judge.

<u>The Defense moves for the admission into the Trial Record each of these photos</u>

<u>Earl Warren: I approve the stipulation as to their proper foundation and their admission.</u>

Did you play a role after the assassination of the president?

Yes.

In what capacity was that?

As the Acting U.S. Attorney General, I approved the disposal into a depth of nine thousand feet in the Atlantic Ocean of the bronze casket that carried the corpse of president JFK from Dallas to Washington, D.C.

How did your approval arise?

Senator Robert Kennedy of New York requested the destruction of this property so that it would not become a public curiosity.

Were there other attempts on the president's life prior to Dealey Plaza?

There are three known attempts on the president's life in the fall of 1963. Thomas Arthur Vallee, a JFK hater and right-wing extremist, was arrested by the U.S. Secret Service in Chicago just days before the president was to speak. Vallee had stockpiled an M1 rifle, a handgun, and three thousand rounds of ammunition.

Days Later, the Secret Service received another threat to the president to be ambushed also in Chicago by a Cuban hit squad. On November 18, 1963, Miami right winger, Joseph Milteer, outlined to police informant, William M. Somersett, the details of an assassination attempt in Dallas.

A military man patsy was identified to take the rap in Chicago.

Was the Abraham Zapruder film of the assassination, showing the head of the president forced backwards from a frontal wound, suppressed?

The Zapruder film was kept from public scrutiny for twelve years. On March 6, 1975, the Zapruder footage was passed to TV journalist Geraldo Rivera by political activist Dick Gregory and conspiracy theorist, Robert Grodin. Grodin was the photographic consultant to the House Select Committee on Assassination and a technical adviser on Oliver Stone's movie, "JFK."

Rivera aired the footage on his show, "Good Night, America." David B. Nolan, former White House attorney, appeared on Geraldo at Large in January 2010 on behalf of US. Supreme Court appellant, Karen Sypher.

Zapruder reiterated four times during his Warren Commission" testimony that he believed shots came from behind him, not from the Texas School Book Depository to his left.

Did Chief Justice Earl Warren first refuse the request by President Lyndon Baines Johnson to head an investigation into the murder of President Kennedy?

Yes.

When was the Warren Commission report released?

September 27, 1964. This was more than ten months after the JFK assassination.

Are there multiple identities to and for Lee Harvey Oswald?

Oswald had two military identification cards in his possession: one in his name and one for "Alek J. Hidell," when arrested in Dallas.

The Mannlicher-Carbano rifle had been dropped off for a scope sighting by a "Hidell." Lee Harvey Oswald was thought to be in Mexico City when the rifle was dropped for site reconfiguration.

Did the same bullet hit both the president and Governor Connally?

No. Spectrographic testing of the fragments from Governor Connally's wrist is not consistent with copper jacketed bullets linked to the Mannlicher-Carcano rifle. Thus, there is no single rifle at Dealey Plaza on November 22, 1963.

The telescopic sight on the Mannlicher-Carbano was set for a left-handed shooter. Oswald is a rightie.

Has there been a finger print match taken from the 6th floor at Texas School Book Depository?

Yes, there is a match for Malcolm "Mac" Wallace. Wallace was convicted of murdering a golf pro who was an intimate of Lyndon Baines Johnson's sister, Josefa. Wallace is associated with several other LBJ linked murders besides that of LBJ's sister, an alleged prostitute.

Was there a finger or palm print of Lee Harvey Oswald on the Mannlicher -Carcano rifle found on the fifth floor of the Book Depository?

No. Moreover, there was no gun powder residue on Oswald either.

Were other rifles found in the upper floors of the Texas School Book Depository?

Yes. Both a Mauser and a British Enfield rifle were found on the sixth floor of the Texas School Book Depository. Each of these is a more accurate weapon for snipers.

Is there any evidence that Oswald ever purchased ammunition for the Mannlicher-Carcano?

No.

Is there any evidence that Oswald owned gun maintenance supplies for the Mannlicher-Carcano rifle?

No. However, the alleged murder weapon was recently oiled before November 22, 1963.

Who approved the final presidential motorcade route?

Dallas Police Chief, Jesse Curry, approved the motorcade route in conjunction with Secret Service agents, Winston Lawson and Forrest Sorrels. Curry attended the FBI academy and kissed up to powerful Texas men such as LBJ to obtain and stay in power. The route was announced October 16, 1963 and published in the Dallas Times Mirror for public consumption. This notice resulted in a one- half million member crowd along the presidential motorcade.

The motorcade route chosen by Curry and the U.S. Secret Service furthered the vulnerability for assassination. The Dal-Tex Building and the Texas School Book Depository Building had open windows for snipers as buildings surrounding the Dealey Plaza. There were no escape or alternative routes from the Dealey Plaza.

Dallas police were told to face away from open windows and the ten deep crowds along the motorcade route. Moreover, there were no Dallas police officers stationed around the Dealey Plaza. Only a couple of escorting police motorcycles was there to protect the president. One radio was left on continuously and recorded more than three rifle shots.

Is there a 1947 memo written by an FBI assistant that says that "one Jack Rubenstein of Chicago is performing services for the staff of Congressman Richard Nixon of California?

Yes.

Is each assertion in the Defense opening statement correct to the best of your knowledge?

Yes.

Fourth Defense Witness: T Hale Boggs

Please state your name for the record.

T. Hale Boggs, House Majority Leader

Did you make a statement regarding the Kennedy assassination?

The FBI provided me dirty files on individuals who questioned the Warren Commission findings.

Fifth Defense Witness: Orville Nix

Please state your name for the record?

Orville Nix.

Do you have a record to authenticate concerning the assassination of the president?

My film footage from the Dealey Plaza features suspicious flashes from the grassy knoll that could have resulted in the frontal entry gun shots into the president's neck and brain.

The Warren Commission claimed that these images were from a shadow of a tree branch that disappears in later frames.

Sixth Defense Witness: Robert Hughes

Please state your name and occupation for the record?

Robert Hughes. I am a Canadian journalist.

Do you have a record to authenticate concerning the assassination of the president?

My 8mm film captured the movement of two individuals between the top two, corner windows of the 6h Floor of the Texas School Book Depository Building. My print of the Texas School Book Depository on November 22, 1963 shows a barrel extending over a windowsill and two figures poised above it.

Seventh Defense Witness: Beverly Oliver

Please state your name for the record?

Beverly Oliver.

What do you know about the assassination of the president?

I was a nineteen-year-old employee of Jack Ruby's strip club, the Carousel, on November 22, 1963. Two individuals claiming to be government officials took my film from my new Yashuica movie camera. My footage from the Dealey Plaza was never returned.

Eighth Defense Witness: Richard Russell

Please state your name and JFK assassination roll for the record?

I am U.S. Senator Richard Russell of Georgia, a member of the Warren Commission

What is your statement about the assassination of the JFK?

I refuse to accept the single bullet theory that a single bullet both struck President Kennedy and then smashed into Governor John Connally's wrist.

Ninth Defense Witness: John Sherman Cooper

Please state your name and JFK assassination roll for the record?

 I am U.S. Senator John Sherman Cooper of Kentucky and a Warren Commission member.

What is your statement about the assassination of the president?

There is no evidence that the same men, i.e. President Kennedy and Governor Connally, were hit by the same bullet."

Tenth Defense Witness: Boris Yeltsin

Please stat your name for the record.

Boris Yeltsin

What do you know about the assassination of the president?

In June 1999 as the Russian president, I hand delivered to President Bill Clinton a package of eighty documents compiled by my KGB throughout the cold war years and recently declassified. These records reflect that the nineteen -year old Oswald entered the Soviet Union on a six-day visa. Four years later, these documents refute many of the U.S. government's bogus explanations.

Memos were circulated among the USSR deputy premier, the Soviet Foreign Minister, and the head of the KGB that announced Oswald's arrival. Oswald was provided with a job, an apartment, a five thousand dollar furniture allowance, and seven hundred rubles a month in spending money.

My KGB and French Intelligence believe LBJ masterminded the Kennedy assassination.

Eleventh Defense Witness: Saundra Spencer

Please state your name for the record?

Saundra Spencer.

Do you have a view regarding the assassination of the president?

I discovered that there were two sets of photographs regarding the wounds of President Kennedy from November 22, 1963.

The photographs from the final report of the Assassination Records Review Board in September 1998 do not match those in the National Archives since 1966. The former show an entry would in the president's right temple that resulted in a grapefruit size exit wound to the back of his head.

Four autopsy photos are missing and another badly altered.

Twelfth Defense Witness: George Herbert Walker Bush

Please state your name and JFK connection for the record.

George Herbert Walker Bush. I am a former CIA Director under Richard Nixon and a one-term president.

I invaded Iraq.

What is your statement about a conspiracy to murder president Kennedy?

There are people who still think Elvis is alive.

Thirteenth Defense Witness: Gore Vidal

Please state your name and JFK connection for the record?

Gore Vidal. I am an author and step-brother to Jackie Kennedy.

Do you have a statement about JFK's assassination?

Americans have been trained by the media to go into Pavlovian giggles at the mention of "conspiracy" because for an American to believe in a conspiracy he must also believe in flying saucers or craziest of all that more than one person was involved in the JFK murder.

Fourteenth Defense Witness: Jacqueline Bovier Kennedy

Please state your name for the record.

Jacqueline Bovier Kennedy. I am the widow of the deceased president.

What is your view about your husband's murder?

I believe LBJ and Texas businessmen played a role.

French intelligence informed me that LBJ murdered my husband.

Fifteenth Defense Witness: Lyndon Baines Johnson

Please state your name for the record?

Lyndon Baines Johnson

What is your statement about who is responsible for your "accidental" presidency on November 22, 1963?

I was elected Vice President by the American people. I was the natural successor on JFK's death.

In my CBS Reports interview in 1969, I stated, I don't think that they or me or anyone else is always sure of everything that might have motivated Oswald or others that could have been involved. But he was quite a mysterious fellow and he did have connections that bore examination. And the extent of the influence of those connections on him, I think history will deal with much more than we're able to now."

Did you duck and cover when your VP limousine entered the Dealey Plaza?

Yes, I leaned down below the back of the front seat because I was trying to listen better to a walkie talkie on the vehicle floor.

Did you have prescience at that time that snipers awaited the presidential motorcade?

I always believed since I was a boy that someday I would that would become president of the United States.

Are you bi-polar?

Some say I have mood swings between omnipotence and deep depression.

Did you tell your confident, Madeline Brown, that you knew of the Dallas massacre of JFK in advance?

I told her that American Oil men and the CIA ordered the assassination. In anticipation in the following motorcade limousine, I cringed as the first shot was fired at Dealey Plaza.

Did you provide sworn testimony to the Warren Commission about your ducking and covering before shots ranged out?

Hell no, only a written statement. I even had an AP photo of my curious behavior to the Warren Commission cropped because I did not want to show complicity or foreknowledge as to anything. If I wanted to protect myself, wouldn't I have pushed down Lady Bird to protect her from shots for Senator Yarborough?

What was your unsworn Warren Commission statement?

I was startled by sharp report or explosion, but I had no time to speculate as to its origin because Agent Youngblood turned in a flash, immediately after the first explosion, hitting me on the shoulder, and shouted to all of us in the back seat to get down. I was pushed down by Agent Youngblood. Almost in the same moment in which he hit or pushed me, he vaulted over the back seat and sat on me. I was bent over under the weight of Agent Youngblood's body, toward Mrs. Johnson and Senator Yarborough.

Sixteenth Defense Witness: Secret Service Agent, Rufus Youngblood

Were you a Secret Service Agent responsible for protecting the vice presidential limousine in the JFK motorcade on November 22, 1963?

Yes.

Were you behind vice president Johnson when the second shot was heard at the Dealey Plaza?

I can't be certain when I reacted.

I noticed that the movements in the Presidential car were very abnormal and, at practically the same time, the movements in the Presidential follow-up car were abnormal. I turned in my seat and with my left arm grasped and shoved the Vice President, at his right shoulder, down and toward Mrs. Johnson and Senator Yarborough. At the same time, I shouted "get down!" I believe I said this more than once and the other occupants of the rear seat. They all responded very rapidly.

Were you in the AP photo by James "Ike" Altgens shoving down LBJ?

No

Seventeenth Defense Witness: Dallas police officer B.J. Martin

Did the Vice President duck down before the intervention of Secret Service Rufus Youngblood?

According to the guys who were escorting his car, the Vice President started ducking down in the car a good 30 or 40 seconds before the first shot was fired.

Prosecution Objection and Move to Strike: This is hearsay. The sworn statement by officer Martin implies that the Vice President knew in advance that Dealey Plaza was to be the murder zone for the President.

Judge Earl Warren: Objection sustained.

Eighteenth Defense Witness: James "Ike" Altgens

Were you an Associated Press photographer who took attached photo of the limousines of JFK and LBJ entering the Dealey Plaza?

Yes.

What did you observe at this time?

I saw the Vice President ducking for cover before I heard the first shot.

Was your photo cropped to exclude the VP limousine prior to its submission to the Warren Commission?

Yes.

Nineteenth Defense Witness: Ed Hoffman

Please hand sign your name and your other answers for the record?

Ed Hoffman

Were you at the Dealey Plaza on November 22, 1963?

Yes.

What did you observe?

I watched from the triple underpass as two men in dark suits lay in wait for the president with drawn rifles behind the fence on the grassy knoll. I watched them fire and then casually dismantle their weapons. I tried on five occasions to report these observations. The first time was to the Secret

Service, the second time to the Dallas police, and finally to the FBI. No interpreter was ever offered to me as a deaf mute.

Twentieth Defense Witness: Jack Ruby

Please state for the record your name?

Jack Ruby

Have you been known by other names?

Yeah. Jacob Leon Rubenstein.

Do you know the Defendant, Lee Harvey Oswald?

Yeah. He's been in my strip club, the Carousel.

Are you known to be an organized crime figure?

Some say so.

Did you have an association with mobster, Al Capone?

Yeah. As a teenager in Chicago, I ran messages for Al.

Do many police officers attend the Carousel?

Yes. Many are my friends or those of my girls.

Why were there no police officers walking in front of Defendant Oswald in the Police basement?

Maybe they did not want to block the view of the TV cameramen. You would have to ask them.

Why did you shoot Lee Harvey Oswald?

I did not want to have Jackie Kennedy go through the pain of a trial of Oswald. The killing of the president was solved and avenged by me.

Did you know Officer J.D. Tippet?

Yeah, he attended my strip club, Carousel.

Did you know Lee Harvey Oswald before November 22, 1963?

Oswald came to the Carousel Club and participated from the crowd in the magician act of William D. Crowe.

Did you and Oswald meet with members of organized crime five days before the November 22, 1963 events?

Yes.

Have two witnesses identified you as being around the Dealey Plaza on November 22, 1963?

Yes. Julia Ann Mercer claims she saw my unloading weapons from a Ford pickup truck and heading for the grassy knoll. Police officer Tom Tilson of the Dallas police claims to have followed a black car leaving the Dealey Plaza and seen me as its occupant.

Did Evangelist Roy Rushing observe your riding a police elevator, at 9:30 AM, two hours before you shot Oswald?

I don't remember because of my distracting grief on that day.

Do you owe $60,000 in back taxes to the IRS?

Yes.

On the day after the presidential assassination, did you deposit $7,000 in large bills in your savings account?

Yes.

Twenty - First Defense Witness: Lee Harvey Oswald

Please state you name for the record.

Lee Harvey Oswald

Are you an agent of federal government?

Yes, the Office of Naval Intelligence (ONI).

Are all statements in my opening argument and the defense record so far true and correct?

Yes.

Who can confirm that you have been in the past and/or now part of the U.S. Intelligence?

The following professionals at various federal agencies can corroborate my prior and ongoing involvement with U.S. Intelligence. They include:

William R. "Tosh" Plumlee and Richard Case Nagell of U.S. Military Intelligence.

E. Howard Hunt, Victor Marchetti, John Stockwell, James Wilcott, Ronald Augustinovich, Chauncey Holt, David Atlee Phillips, William Morrow, and George De Mohrenschildt of the CIA.

Air Force Colonel L. Fletcher Prouty, a liaison to CIA for Clandestine Operations. He is a composite character in Oliver Stone's movie. "JFK".

William C. Bishop, a Senior Military Officer of Executive Action.

Dr. John M. Newman of the National Security Agency (NSA).

Zack Shelton and William Turner of the FBI, and

Captain Edward Seiwell and Captain Gilbert Cook of the U.S. Army Intelligence.

Did your arrest in Dallas trigger a U.S. military response?

James Hosty of the FBI was considered my "handler" at the time. The United States military went to Defense Condition 3 (DEFCOM3) shortly after my arrest on November 22, 1963. Just before reaching Cuban airspace, these planes were hastily called back.

In conjunction with the launching of this attack, the entire U.S. military went on alert. Fidel Castro and the Soviets were being blamed for the death of the 35th president as further justification for another attempted Cuban invasion after the previous missile crisis.

When did you come to work with or know some of these U.S. government officials?

In spring of 1961, I knew "Tosh" Plumlee from my attachment to "Task Force W" (TFW). This unit was sometimes used a special top-secret strike force for emergency military actions in support of presidential protection and security.

Some TFW operational units were attached directly to the Pentagon. Our dispatches and orders came from deep within the Pentagon, CIA and the National Security Council (NSC) at the White House and directly from the President of the United States.

Did you like intelligence work?

Yes. I loved the spy TV show, I Led Three Lives. My intelligence participation in it made me feel important and proud as an American. It confirmed my ability to contribute to a Cold War victory for the United States. I could also funnel disinformation in Russia to undermine the Soviets and to further U.S. interests. I have a 116 IQ for such work. I am very well read and speak fluent Russian.

Did you attend the so-called Spook School?

Yes. I met "Tosh" at Nag's Head, North Carolina at the Illusionary Warfare training facility known as "Spook School." The curriculum includes propaganda, language instruction, false identities, and maintenance of cover stories.

Were you involved with military intelligence in Texas?

Yes. Captain Seiwell of the Fourth Army Reserve in Dallas and Captain Gilbert C. Cook helped run a special unit connected to 112th Military Intelligence Group (MIG) in Dallas and San Marcos, Texas. They also knew my association with the Office of Naval Intelligence (ONI).

ONI maintained facilities at Bachman's Lake, near Dallas' Love Field. This airport is where the president landed on November 22, 2013.

Were you ordered to infiltrate Soviet Union Intelligence?

Yes.

Who can confirm this fact?

The Executive Assistant to the Deputy Director of the CIA, Victor L. Marchetti.

What was your role in this infiltration?

I was one of three dozen, perhaps as many as forty (40) men, who agreed to appear as disenchanted, poor, American youths who had become turned off and wanted to see what living under Communism was all about. Unlike me, those with less vigorous patriotism and skill lasted often only a few weeks in such a charade.

Our intension was that the Soviet Union or Eastern Europe might recruit one or more of us to be KGB of Russia, East Germany's Stassi or other foreign agents. We could feed the Soviets false information if each of our respective covers was not blown.

We were trained at various naval installations both in the U.S. and abroad. The operation was run out of Nags Head, North Carolina.

Did this espionage scheme have a name?

This scheme was known as "doubling." We aspired to be double agents for U.S. national intelligence in the ongoing Cold War.

Do you hold and continue to hold a top secret Security clearance from the U.S. government?

Yes.

What were your early covert efforts for U.S. Intelligence?

I held a Top Secret clearance as a radar operator to support U2 flights over the Soviet Union from my air base, Marine Air Control, in Atsugi, Japan. This was the main CIA base in the Far East in 1957.

My assignments included consorting with "hostesses" at Queen Bee Night Club in Tokyo. My medical military records for September 16, 1958 reflect that I was treated for contracting gonorrhea in the line of duty. These expensive prostitutes, who were known to pass on false "secrets" to the Soviets, were paid for by the U.S. taxpayer.

Did the U.S. Government also pay for your Russian proficiency?

Yes. In 1959, I undertook advance Russian study at the U.S. Army Monterey School of Languages.

Is matriculation into this school difficult?

Yes. Each student admitted required a future important assignment for U.S. Military Intelligence.

Did you help to break up the May 17, 1960 peace talks that included the USSR and the United States?

Yes.

What happened?

The release of radar information enabled the shooting down of Gary Power's U2 spy plane. This was a pretext for Khrushchev to call off the planned talks because of U.S. "aggressive actions."

Were your communist rants to bystanders and the press regarding "Fair Play for Cuba" part of your calculated "duality" cover?

Yes. I believe in the Marine Corp motto, *Semper Fidelis* to my country.

Did you matriculate to the Albert Schweitzer College in Switzerland to facilitate your entry into Soviet Union?

Yes. However, Helsinki, Finland was the easiest point of entry by train into mother Russia in 1959.

Did you fake grounds for a U.S. Marines "Dependency Discharge"?

Yes. Immediately prior to my Soviet defection, I asserted my mother's injured foot as an emergency. Her medical problem actually occurred six months prior to my discharge.

What did you do to try to infiltrate Soviet Intelligence once in Russia?

I applied but was rejected for admission to the Patrice Lumumba University in Moscow. This is a notorious terrorist incubation center that we wanted to infiltrate.

Did you fake your own suicide attempt in the USSR to avoid deportation back to Finland in 1959?

Yes.

Did the CIA maintain a "201 file" on you confirming that you were a U.S. Intelligence operative in the U.S.S. R.?

Yes.

Did you possess U.S. spy equipment in the USSR?

Yes. I was given a Minox spy camera that is not otherwise commercially available.

Did you have an easy time to re-enter the United States from the Soviet Union?

Yes. Neither my wife Marina nor I were was detained despite my earlier "defection" from the United States I had previously "renounced" my U.S. citizenship at the height of the Cold War. The U.S. government both financed my trip to the Soviet Union and the return of Marina and me to the United States without triggering any obstacles.

Did your wife, Marina Prusaka Oswald, provide you with a Soviet Intelligence cover?

Yes. She was born illegitimate and raised by her uncle, Ilya Prusakova. He was a Colonel in the Ministry of Internal Affairs (MIA), aka Soviet Secret Police. He was also member of the local Communist Party. However, I consider him friendly to U.S. interests.

Marina was able to meet me and one of the other first three "U.S. defectors" in our spy group to the Soviet Union, in cities, hundreds of miles apart. I "married" my teen age bride within days of our first meeting as the favored spouse choice.

At the height of the Cold War tensions, we had no exit difficulties from the Soviet Union. My U.S. passport was returned to me by the U.S. State Department. I received from the U.S. Embassy a promissory note of $435.71 so as to continue my mission. U.S. Intelligence assigned to me George de Mohrenshildt, a Russian émigré and CIA operative, to help perpetuate the sham that I was a Communist sympathizer. George de Mohrenshildt committed suicide immediately before an anticipated visit by journalist Bill O'Reilly.

Did the CIA deny initially the conducting of your intelligence debriefing on your return to America?

Yes. The CIA finally admitted to my debriefing on my return to America.

Shortly before the presidential assassination, did you associate with David Ferrie's ultra-conservative Civil Air Patrol in Texas?

Yes. He is gay, just like the CIA's Clay Shaw, aka Guy Bannister, whom the New Orleans prosecutor, Jim Garrison went after.

Did you leave Fort Worth for Dallas to work for the firm of Jaggers-Chiles and Stovall?

Yes.

What did you do for this firm?

I was a photographic trainee. The firm has a sensitive contract with the U.S. Map Service that provides photographs taken by the U-2 spy planes flying over Cuba.

When did you change work to the Texas School Book Depository?

October 16, 1963, just as the motorcade route was being imposed for November 21 or 22.

Were you part of an effort to investigate rogue elements of the federal government?

Yes.

Who can corroborate this fact?

On November 22, 2013, Tosh Plumlee and our intell team split in three directions so as to look for snipers or sniper teams for suspected triangulated fire at the most vulnerable location on the presidential motorcade route.

Were you part of an effort to deter the planned assassination of President Kennedy?

Yes.

Who can corroborate this fact?

Tosh Plumlee and our intell team. We were looking for snipers or teams of snipers in a triangulation along the parade route in Dallas.

Did you concentrate on any specific location?

Yes. Dealey Plaza at Elm and Houston Streets in Dallas.

Why was this an excellent location for a triangulation of snipers?

The Dallas Police Chief Curry did not place patrolmen on sidewalks so as to control bystanders at the Dealey Plaza. He further ordered his policemen to face the motorcade rather than the crowd and open windows along the path of a motorcade from where a sniper's rifle might be observed.

In order to pretend that there was a lone assassin, a rifle barrel distraction was deliberately made viewable from the 6th Floor of the School Book Depository to garner interest away from the other firing sites. If it were I at this location to assassinate, I would not have been so stupid as literally to tip my hand by letting my weapon be seen before aiming and firing.

Do you fear death from another attempted assassination by a successor to mobster Jacob Rubenstein, aka Jack Ruby?

Yes. This trial has compromised the U.S. Intelligence community. I am likely a dead man in a deliberate cover up of my failure and that of others to stop this assignation attempt as in the other attempts, three months prior to November 22, 1963.

Why would anyone want to kill you?

Rogue elements of the Dallas Police, who were acquaintances of Ruby at his Carousel Club strip joint, botched their attempt to kill me at the Texas movie theatre and later at Dallas police headquarters at my press conference the night before that Ruby attended. The Mafia ordered their low level flunky Ruby to kill me or he would be a dead man if the Mafia conspiracy of shooters unraveled with my trial. Ruby knew that he was already dying of cancer and was a walking dead man himself who had nothing to lose since the legal system would never quickly execute him with Melvin Belli as his high powered defense attorney. Ruby came to my press conference but had cold feet to shoot until the next morning.

Did you murder officer Tippet during your travel from your apartment to the Texas Movie Theater?

No. I never ever met Officer Tippet. I have no motive to hurt him and draw attention to myself. I was deliberately framed to make it appear that I am a violent person.

Why should you be believed?

Police records reflect that Officer J.D. Tippit was murdered by four bullets from an automatic pistol. I do not own or have access to an automatic pistol. I only own and carry my 38 caliber revolver for my personal protection in my infiltration of the assassination cabal.

Tippet's body and car was found seven blocks to the east of my direct cab route from my apartment towards my Movie Theater rendezvous. I had no reason to divert my cab from that direct route for my planned meeting with my doppelganger "Harvey Oswald" at the movie theater.

Were there other federal government operatives in Dallas with knowledge to stop the assassination of JFK?

Yes. We suspected that the assassination of JFK likely would be staged from a triangulation around the Dealey Plaza.

Is that why you sought work at the Texas School Book Depository at Dealey Plaza?

Yes. I began stuffing book boxes at the Depository for $1.25 an hour on November 16, 1963.

Who could have called off the assassination of JFK?

Mobster Sam Giancana from Chicago. He chanced going forward because he probably assessed that the U.S. Intelligence community was highly compromised to admit that rogue federal elements were involved to assassinate the president. Even Bobby Kennedy would fear taking on both the FBI and CIA until he could be elected president after his brother.

Where were you when the JFK limousine approached the Dealey Plaza?

I was sipping a Coke in the second floor lunch room at the School Book Depository.

Did anyone observe you at this location on November 22, 2013?

Yes. My boss, Roy Truly, and Dallas Motorcycle patrolman, Marion Baker, saw me at this location around 1:00 PM.

Were you later photographed on the side walk outside the Depository around the time when the JFK limousine actually passed by completely?

Yes.

Is there any photographic or other evidence of your being seen from any of 20,000 windows along the parade route?

No.

Is there any powder residue on your cheek or fingerprints identifying you to the Manlicher -Carbano or other rifle found at the 6th floor of the School Book Repository?

No.

Is there a doctored photograph distributed showing your holding a rifle?

Yes.

Are you a good shooter?

My fellow Marines made fun of my weak marksmanship. They would laugh when a "Maggie's drawers" flag would go up when I missed a target on a shooting range. My erratic shooting led to my derogatory nick name, "Shitfit."

Through persistence, I eventually obtained an intermediate marksmanship ranking with still targets while a U.S. Marine. I am unable to hit a moving target.

Were you recruited as a sniper?

Yes. For the Fidel Castro assassination team, not for those colluding to kill President Kennedy from far range as a moving target.

Would you have chosen to use the Mannlicher-Carbano rifle in the assassination of anyone?

No. For fewer than twenty dollars, I bought a year 1940 Manlicher-Carbano, a World War I surplus rifle, for target practice. I wanted to maintain adequate shooting skills for the kill Castro, "Mongoose" operation, in Cuba. I was eventually approved for a visa to Cuba to assist in killing the communist Cuban dictator.

After assuming power, Castro killed 20,000 of his countrymen. The Diem brothers, removed by President Kennedy, killed 50,000 of theirs.

Are you a haughty or arrogant person?

My wife says that I am sometimes. Some have accused me of grandiose thoughts about my abilities and destiny. I call it self-confidence from my ongoing modest successes in the intelligence field. I only attempt to show humility when it serves my purpose.

Aren't you a high school drop out?

Yes. I left an unhappy single parent home to join patriotically the U.S. Marines as a teenager. Similarly, Jack Kennedy did not finish his studies at Stanford University Business School after his Harvard degree despite having more than enough family money to continue his studies.

Unlike the JFK, I have never had enough money to earn a college degree or even to buy a car.

Do you read extensively?

Yes. I consider myself at age twenty-four to be relatively well-read. I have read the ghost-written Profiles in Courage and the biography of the John Kennedy, *Portrait of a President,* by William Manchester. I avidly read domestic city newspapers and socialist worker publications.

Did you hate or even dislike JFK?

No. I have no motive to hurt the president Kennedy.

However, many in the Mafia, CIA, FBI and Naval Intelligence feel that JFK showed no back bone in negligently failing to provide enough aerial support to make the Bay of Pigs invasion successful to overthrow Castro. Many see his selling out to the agenda of Rev. Martin Luther King on civil rights.

The president set himself up to be murdered when he fired CIA Director, Allen Dulles, in October 1963. I believe that the president wanted to weaken the CIA as a pretext to have his brother Bobby reorganize the agency over after the expected 1964 election victory.

I have little interest in such power struggles. They should not affect my U.S. intelligence officer career.

Did you learn Russian from your wife Marina?

No. I completed my Russian proficiency at the U.S. Government's language school in Monterey, California. Matriculation there is highly selective. My acceptance confirms that the top federal Russian language training was needed for my key intelligence objectives. I helped translate Russian from U2 photographs when I worked for my Dallas contractor for the U.S. Mapping Agency and the CIA.

Is your wife Marina a possible KGB agent?

No. However, she was raised by her uncle whom I believe was a double agent for many years. Marina likes America and wants to remain here to raise our daughters, June and Audrey. She supported my decision to take our family back to America from the Soviet Union. She does not want to return to the USSR.

Do you still possess both a valid USSR and a U.S. passport?

Yes.

Why was JFK in Dallas on November 22, 1963?

I believe he was there for political "fence mending" with alienated Democratic party members who did not like the failure of the Bay of Pigs invasion of Cuba fiasco and his tacit support of Martin Luther King's fight for civil rights. Senator Yarborough leads the left wing of the party in Texas. LBJ is out for himself.

President Kennedy also had many enemies with "Big Oil" for wishing to eliminate the oil depletion allowance and those who would profit from an expanded Viet Nam War armament production. They did not like his 1963 decision to begin to return the U.S. advisors and troops from the Diem government in South Viet Nam. They were surprised by the coup to assassinate the Catholic Diem brothers from fighting a communist takeover from the Viet Minh and North Vietnam.

Was the Dallas area a hostile political area for the president?

Yes. Around sixty-three percent of Dallas voters rejected President Kennedy in 1960.

Many of my neighbors and friends hate the president. Car bumper strips here state, "K.O. the Kennedys."

A local poster of Kennedy is designed to look like a mug shot that bears the inscription, "Wanted for Treason-This Man is Wanted for Treasonous Activities Against the United States." I assume this would include the promise not to invade Cuba after the missile crisis.

Is Dallas, Texas a dangerous city?

There are more murders committed in Texas than that of any other state. There are more Dallas homicides than that of any other Texas location.

Texas does not register or otherwise regulate any firearm. Seventy-two percent of Texas murders are by gunshot.

From where was the kill-shot to JFK?

It came from the front of the presidential limousine and behind the fence at the grassy knoll.

Where were you at this time?

I was at the rear and other end of the president's motorcade.

How do we know that there were shots from the front of the limousine?

Dozens of observers witnessed the President's head being driven backward forcibly from the impact of the frontal shot to his forehead.

Emergency room doctors and their records confirm an additional frontal entry wound in the President's throat and right temple. This hole was used for a tracheotomy to help the president's troubled breathing before his heart stopped.

Even if I were a shooter at the Texas School Book Depository, I could not have inflicted either of the two frontal wounds to the president.

What physical evidence is there of frontal shots to JFK?

Motorcycle officers, Bobby Hargis and B.J. Martin flanked the president's limousine from the left rear. Their windshields were spattered with large amounts of the president's blood and brain matter from the fatal shot from the right-front of the limousine originating in the shooter's nest behind the fence at the grassy knoll.

Do witnesses confirm your conclusion of frontal shots?

Yes. Over one hundred witnesses confirm seeing or hearing at least one shot from the grassy knoll just above street level. Twenty-five persons smelled gun powder and/or saw rifle smoke near the fence on the grassy knoll immediately in front of the railroad overpass.

Do you have a C2766 bolt-action 6.5 Mannlicher-Carcano rifle, Model 91/38?

Yes, through the mail order under the alias name of Alek J. Hidell.

Is this a World War I surplus weapon?

Yes.

Is it a good weapon for a sniper?

No. This is a 1940 imprecise weapon bought for fewer than twenty dollars through mail order. It is an Italian piece of surplus junk.

It is an unprofessional choice for sniping because each successive bolt action shot is time consuming and difficult to re-aim. After the first shot, the potential for hitting a target is severely limited, especially with a target trailing away as the presidential limousine did. My modern M-1 rifles from the Marines spoiled me. They similarly use copper-jacketed military ammunition.

The site on my Mannlicher-Carcano is inaccurate. This rifle is not reliable. They are best used for a warning shot to the street, such as in an attempt to thwart the timing of triangulated snipers.

Is the 6th Floor window of the Book Deposit Building a good choice for a sniper?

No. The angles are very poor with trees blocking the sight of much of the kill zone.

Where are the better sites at the Dealey Plaza?

Chicago Mafiosi, James Files and Chuck Nicoletti, would be better positioned at the Dal-Tex building or the grassy knoll. Unlike the Depository, there are no trees to block a sniper's vision from an upper floor of the Dal-Tex building or the grassy knoll fence.

The Dal-Tex building is across Houston Street from the School Book Depository. Chuck Nicoletti is regarded as the top mafia sniper from either location.

On November 22, 1963, was Chuck Nicoletti stationed at the Dal-Tex building at Dealey Plaza or the grassy knoll?

Yes. John Rosselli was possibly with him. Tosh Plumlee was a CIA pilot who flew Roselli to Dallas that morning.

Were snipers stationed at the grassy knoll?

Yes. The grassy knoll closely overlooks Elm Street. It is only thirty feet from the presidential limousine when it slows to make a turn under the railroad bridge overpass. It is a turkey shoot for any sniper to make a fatal head shot from this location.

Charles Harrelson and Charles Rogers, aka Richard Montoya, were stationed at the grassy knoll. They were detained for questioning by the Dallas motorcycle cops and then curiously released as tramps.

Were there at least two types of bullet fragments recovered with different loads, weights and contents in the Dealey Plaza shootings of the president?

Yes. Unlike the other weapons at the Dealey Plaza, the Mannlicher-Carbano only shoots military bullets with copper jacketing. The first shot from such a weapon missed and allegedly hit the street.

This weapon was sarcastically called the "peacemaker" in WWI because of its reputation for its poor ability to hit accurately targets. The differing bullet types from different trajectories confirm multiple weapons and shooters. The fatal shot to the president's forehead was a "frangible" bullet, known as a "hot load" or exploding bullet. It caused a devastating injury to the president's skull as it fragmented.

Is the Mannlicher-Carbano carbine a high- velocity weapon?

No. Its muzzle velocity is only 2,000 feet per second (fps). The president's autopsy report declared that the damage to the president's skull was from a high-velocity bullet of at least 2,600 fps.

Do medical reports confirm nearly simultaneous shots from to the president's body from both behind and front?

Yes. Any two such closely spaced shots are incompatible with a single gunman firing a bolt action Mannlicher-Carbano rifle. There were too many shots, too close together, with different types of bullets to be the work of a single shooter.

What was the result of the police paraffin test for gun fire residue on you after arrest?

It was negative. There was no evidence of any fire arm activity on my body on November 22, 1963.

Did the FBI find your fingerprints on the Mannlice3r-Carbano or any of the two other rifles found on the Texas School Book Depository Building?

No.

What was your U.S. Military Intelligence code name?

Alek J. Hidell.

For what purpose did you use this name?

I made false business cards for myself as the president of the Fair Play for Cuba Committee.

Did you get press from this charade?

Yes.

Did other U.S. intelligence members use this code name?

Yes.

Who are responsible for the assassination of and cover up of the murder of John F. Kennedy?

Who has no responsibility? The American public must first ascertain who benefitted to take the risk that an assassination conspiracy could take decades to unravel slowly.

LBJ became the world's most powerful politician after losing power as majority leader in the U.S. Senate to become vice president. The Mafia benefited to get Bobby Kennedy off the back of organized crime. The mobster snipers got paid.

Rogue elements of the CIA and FBI kept the president and Bobby Kennedy from cleaning house at their respective agencies. The Anti-Castro community got revenge for the Bay of Pigs fiasco for which they blamed the president for 110 fatalities and the incarceration of 1200 in Castro's prisons. Dallas police strengthened its alliance with now president Johnson.

Who was mad at the president?

The president fired CIA Director, Allen Dulles in October 1963. Kennedy undermined the over throw of communism In Cuba in the Bay of Pigs disaster and betrayed NATO by removing missiles from Turkey after the Cuban missile crisis.

JFK wanted to install his brother Bobby as the head of the CIA after the 1964 presidential election. The president also wanted to remove J. Edgar Hoover as the head of the FBI who had the goods on the entire Kennedy family prior including Joe Kennedy Sr.'s bootlegging during Prohibition.

What is your role today in the Kennedy assassination?

I am a patsy for two murders. I will probably not be allowed to live long enough to exonerate my name in my trial and appeal. I want my daughters, June and Audrey, to know that I was framed in order to put a lid on the concerted conspiracy to murder a sitting president. My only regret is that I and others failed to stop this crime of the century.

It may take a half century or more for enough of the principals of this cabal to die of natural or other causes before the American public is allowed to learn the truths that I now proffer for history.

What is the context of the presidential assassination?

President Dwight Eisenhower in his farewell address warned about the growth in power of the Military Industrial Complex. As a West Point graduate and World War II leader, he recognized the threat that the ongoing American war machine that helped bring him to power could skew the independence and integrity of the Executive, Legislative, and Judicial branches in violation of the U.S. Constitution.

Jack Kennedy was elected as president with a slim margin of about one vote per precinct. His fatal visit to Texas in November 1963 was to repair his 1964 ties with Texas businessmen and moderate Democrats who have no love for expanded civil rights for minorities. His fatal selection of the ambitious Lyndon John in 1960 as his running mate may have sealed the Catholic New Englander's ultimate doom as a trade for a narrow but key victory in carrying the numerous electoral votes of Texas.

Former Senate Majority Leader, Lyndon Johnson, wanted his vice presidency as a stepping stone over that of his younger running mate and political rival for Democratic Party control. Johnson was ruthless his entire political career. "Discovered" ballots led to his election to the U.S. Senate by a margin of fewer than seventy (70) votes in the populous state of Texas.

The U.S. Central Intelligence Agency did not trust Kennedy after he failed to approve adequate U.S. air support in the Bay of Pigs invasion of Cuba. This invasion had been approved initially by Eisenhower.

Kennedy's ultimate withdrawal of Russian missiles in Cuba was tied to the removal of the U.S. missile threat to the USSR from NATO missiles in Turkey. I served in the U.S. air base which led U2 high altitude flights over the Soviet Union out of concern of the growing military threat of the Russian Bear.

The Military Industrial Complex did not like Kennedy's decision just weeks before his murder to withdraw U.S. advisors to the government of South Vietnam. There were lots of profits to be made by sending hundreds of thousand s of troops to support the corrupt South Vietnamese government.

Upon his assuming the powers of Commander in Chief, Johnson reversed the Kennedy decision to withdraw the U.S. from the Vietnam Civil War. This civil war occurred because President Eisenhower broke his promise of holding national elections that would have likely put war hero Ho Shi Ming in power after the French Indo China war of independence.

Most importantly, President Kennedy planned his own "CIA coup d'état" to reorganize this U.S. Central Intelligence Agency. After the president allowed the murder of the Catholic Ngu brothers in South Vietnam, he wanted his young brother, Robert F. Kennedy to leave as his U.S. Attorney General plum job to lead the reformulated CIA after the 1964 elections. For someone like George H.W. Bush, the CIA could be a stepping stone to the U.S. Presidency.

The mafia did not like Robert Kennedy because of his building his reformer political resume by fighting organized crime, just like New York Governor, Thomas Dewey did. The president's father, Joe Kennedy, had reported mob ties from his money making success by importing Canadian whiskey throughout the Prohibition era near the Kennedy compound in Hyannis Port, Massachusetts.

Was there a plan for you to reach a contact in the event of trouble?

Yes.

I was to meet my doppelganger "Harvey Oswald" at the Texas Movie Theater. Unlike me, my doppelganger is a native born Russian speaker.

Who was Harvey Oswald?

This intelligence operative was in Russia while I was infiltrating anti-Castro Cubans in Florida. This deception failed when Jacob Rubinstein, aka Jack Ruby, failed to assassinate me in the garage of the Dallas police station. Ruby was also allowed to be present at my midnight press conference before my morning departure from the garage at the Dallas jail.

Did you further your own death warrant as a patsy for the conspiracy to kill the president?

Yes. My youngest daughter Audrey was only born on October 20, 1963. She will never know her father.

What was this error?

From the Dallas jail, I made an untraceable phone call for my "cut-out" intermediary contact to my federal case officer. It became clear to me that I was being set up as a powerless fall guy with no financial resources to defend myself legally other than tell the truth at trial.

I have been trained to not blow my intelligence cover, even under torture. However, I took the chance to go over the dam on the chance it might save the life of the father of June and Audrey.

Were you deliberately placed in a false light?

Yes. The CIA was spawning a web of deception about me weeks before the president's murder. I was identified in New Zealand as the presidential sniper before the first shot was fired in Dealey Plaza.

Johnny Rosselli may have actually attempted to thwart the Military Intelligence "Abort Team" by making it known that the "game was up." He was flown into Dallas by CIA pilot, Tosh Plumlee.

It may take a half-century when most of the principals are dead for the plot to discredit me to unravel.

Defense Final Argument

The prosecution has failed to address key issues required for conviction. I request judicial notice of the following out of court statements which shed light on this trial:

Lynette "Squeaky" Fromm said:

Anybody can kill anybody.

The president's brother, Robert Kennedy said upon learning of his brother's murder said:

I thought that they would get one of us, but Jack, after all that he has been through, never worried about it. I thought it would be me.

In 1964, Bertrand Russell, stated:

There has never been a more subversive, conspiratorial, unpatriotic, or endangering course for the United States to hide the truth behind the murder of its recent president.

New Orleans District Attorney, Jim Garrison, stated:

We'll probably end with a curious situation in which most of the thinking people in the country recognize that reality is really quite different from the history the government is announcing.

The failings of the Warren Commission will forever taint the reputation of Chief Justice Earl Warren and the credibility of the Supreme Court itself as above politics. President Eisenhower himself regretted appointing the California politician, Gov. Earl Warren, to be entrusted as the Chief Judge of the U.S. Supreme Court.

The legacy of the Warren Commission taints each justice's ability to address courageously Constitutional questions that have dramatic political consequences. This failure of this Court's intestinal fortitude will likely continue.

Lee Harvey Oswald lacked finances and a single ally to challenge being framed as the sole assassin of President Kennedy. Oswald was the patsy of political powers that, *ultra vires to* the U.S. Constitution, removed President Kennedy from power with impunity. The assassination of President Kennedy is the crime of U.S. history and our nation's most shameful episode.

The wheels of justice through trial reached each of the conspirators to the assassination of President Abraham Lincoln. The same cannot be said for those responsible for the murder of John F. Kennedy.

On the plane to Dallas, the president Kennedy told Congressman Gonzalez, "Henry, **the Secret Service told me they had taken care of everything. There's nothing to worry about.**" The Secret Service changed the motorcade route to go through the Dealey Plaza where sniper nests awaited and the presidential limousine slowed to fewer than ten miles an hour.

The Secret Service diminished the president's limousine shield from eight agents (four on each side) to four (two on each side). After the president grasps his throat from a frontal shot, four assigned Secret Service agents make no move to shield further gun fire. Only Clint Hill, an agent brought in at the last minute by the First Lady, responds quickly to help. The limousine driver, William Greer, slows the vehicle to nearly a standstill.

The Secret Service maintained a list of more than a million people who posed a potential threat to President Kennedy. Though Oswald was known to the CIA, FBI and military intelligence, his name was not on the list.

Senator Richard Schweiker has stated:

There is no longer any reason to have faith in the Warren Commission's picture of the Kennedy assassination. Oswald would be entitled to a new trial based upon the FBI and CIA cover-up.

The assassination of the president and its following cover up is an adverse turning point in American history away from Constitutional government. No longer would Congress use its powers to declare or end wars. The CIA's wars in Viet Nam, Granada, Panama, Iraq, and Afghanistan have each followed.

The LBJ expansion of the Viet Nam War was inevitable to favor the Military Industrial Complex. The United States continued to be the provocateur around the world and in the Middle East, in particular, with equally outrageous inventions such as Iraq's weapons of mass destruction.

In violation of the right to privacy, the Patriot Act would justify government eavesdropping of over one hundred million Americans and deploying assassination drones. U.S. citizens would be targeted for assassination without due process of law beyond U.S. borders.

The Military Industrial Complex through federal and state courts would illegally extend presidential authority and skew Executive Branch succession to those with CIA ties. The American press now perpetuates big lies instead of being Thomas Jefferson's safeguard in defense of democracy.

CBS anchor Dan Rather curiously declared that the Zapruder film confirmed that the kick back of JFK's head was not the result of a high-powered rifle shot from the front. When journalist Bill O'Reilly came to George de Morhrenschildt's home, the CIA's protector of the Oswalds, committed suicide with a shot gun.

If President Kennedy was not safe from rogue elements of government power, who is? Seventy-seven known witnesses to the Kennedy murder or as to aspects of a plot against the president died under bizarre or unexpected circumstances within years of November 22, 1963.

The LBJ precedent is for future presidents to commit crimes to gain power. Once in power they will further government cronyism for their contributors, start wars for the Military Industrial Complex, abuse the power of all federal agencies, appoint crocked judges and agency heads to protect them, and use the IRS and bar officials to go after their perceived enemies.

The Defense Rests

....

Judge Earl Warren

Upon quick but due consideration of my Trial Record, this Court rules that the Defendant is **Guilty** as charged. He is to be put to death by military drone outside the territorial confines of the United States. His body is to slide into the ocean.

There is no appeal from my decision or that of my Warren Commission report. Key documents remain under seal until year 2015.

Printed in the United States
By Bookmasters